GRAPHIC NOVEL J F SKY V.5
 1880 3950   3-22-17   FTB
Aaron, Jason,

Skywalker strikes
                SDW

SKYWALKER STRIKES: VOLUME 5

*It is a period of renewed hope for the Rebellion.
The evil Galactic Empire's greatest weapon, the
Death Star, has been destroyed by the young
rebel pilot Luke Skywalker.*

*But Skywalker knows he has a long way to go if
he ever hopes to become a true Jedi. Seeking
clues to his destiny, he has returned home to
Tatooine.*

*Meanwhile, Darth Vader is seeking answers of
his own and has hired the notorious bounty
hunter Boba Fett to track down the pilot who
destroyed the Death Star....*

JASON AARON
Writer

JOHN CASSADAY
Artist

LAURA MARTIN
Colorist

CHRIS ELIOPOULOS
Letterer

CASSADAY & MARTIN
Cover Artists

HEATHER ANTOS
Assistant Editor

JORDAN D. WHITE
Editor

C.B. CEBULSKI
Executive Editor

AXEL ALONSO
Editor In Chief

JOE QUESADA
Chief Creative Officer

DAN BUCKLEY
Publisher

For Lucasfilm:
Creative Director MICHAEL SIGLAIN
Senior Editor JENNIFER HEDDLE
Lucasfilm Story Group RAYNE ROBERTS, PABLO HIDALGO,
LELAND CHEE

ABDO
Spotlight

ABDOPUBLISHING.COM

Reinforced library bound edition published in 2017 by Spotlight,
a division of ABDO, PO Box 398166, Minneapolis, Minnesota 55439.
Spotlight produces high-quality reinforced library bound editions for
schools and libraries. Published by agreement with Marvel Characters, Inc.

Printed in the United States of America, North Mankato, Minnesota.
042016
092016

THIS BOOK CONTAINS
RECYCLED MATERIALS

marvelkids.com

STAR WARS © & TM 2016 LUCASFILM LTD.

PUBLISHER'S CATALOGING IN PUBLICATION DATA

Names: Aaron, Jason, author. | Cassaday, John ; Martin, Laura, illustrators.
Title: Star Wars : Skywalker strikes / by Jason Aaron ; illustrated by Laura Martin
    and John Cassaday.
Description: Minneapolis, MN : Spotlight, [2017] | Series: Star Wars : Skywalker
    strikes
Summary: Luke Skywalker and the ragtag rebels opposing the Galactic Empire are
    fresh off their biggest victory so far-the destruction of the massive Death Star!
    But the Empire's not toppled yet! Join Luke, Princess Leia, Han Solo,
    Chewbacca, C-3PO, R2-D2, and the rest of the Rebel Alliance as they fight for
    freedom against Darth Vader and his evil master, the Emperor!
Identifiers: LCCN 2016932364 | ISBN 9781614795278 (v.1 : lib. bdg.) | ISBN
    9781614795285 (v.2 : lib. bdg.) | ISBN 9781614795292 (v.3 : lib. bdg.) | ISBN
    9781614795308 (v.4 : lib. bdg.) | ISBN 9781614795315 (v.5 : lib. bdg.) | ISBN
    9781614795322 (v.6 : lib. bdg.)
Subjects: LCSH: Skywalker, Luke (Fictitious character)--Juvenile fiction. | Star Wars
    fiction--Comic books, strips, etc.--Juvenile fiction. | Graphic novels--Juvenile
    fiction.
Classification: DDC 741.5--dc23
LC record available at http://lccn.loc.gov/2016932364

Spotlight

A Division of ABDO
abdopublishing.com

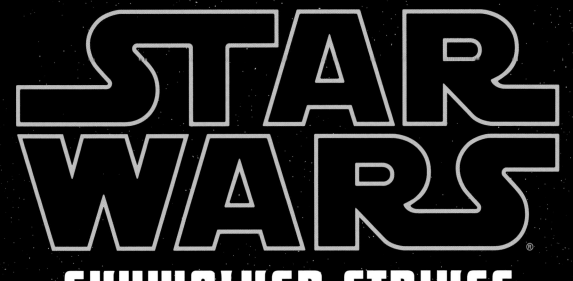

STAR WARS®

SKYWALKER STRIKES

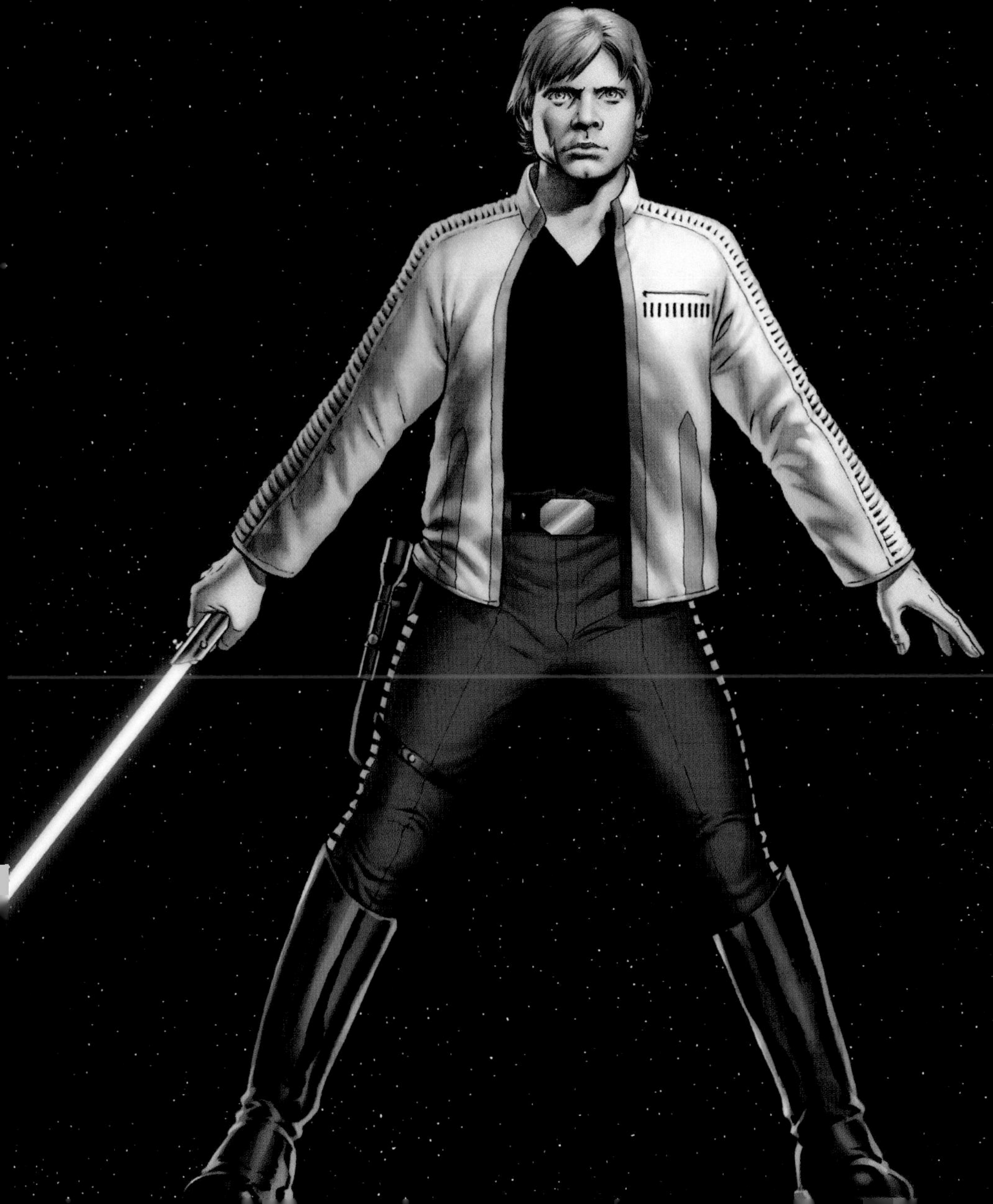

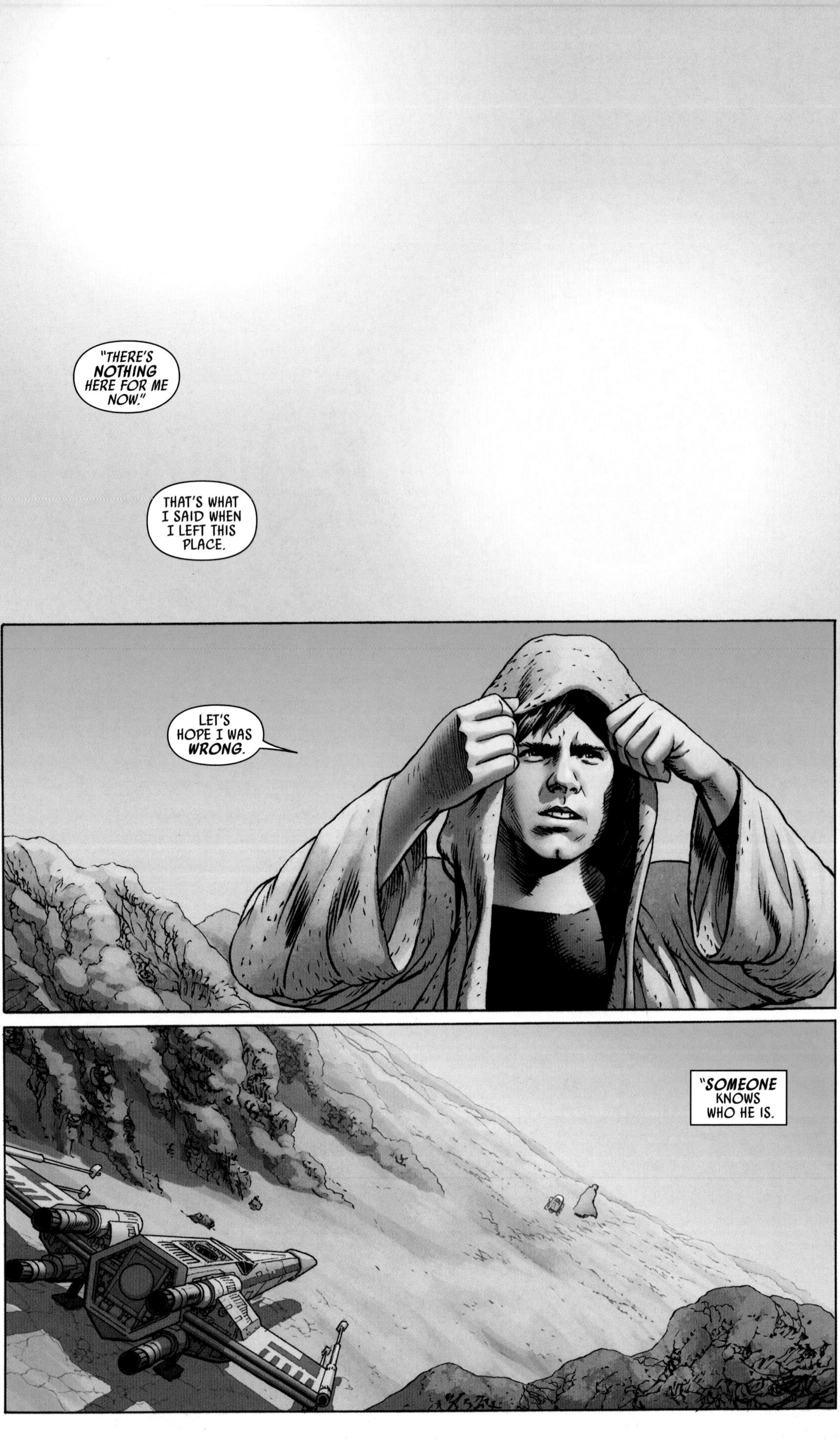
"THERE'S NOTHING HERE FOR ME NOW."
THAT'S WHAT I SAID WHEN I LEFT THIS PLACE.
LET'S HOPE I WAS WRONG.
"SOMEONE KNOWS WHO HE IS.

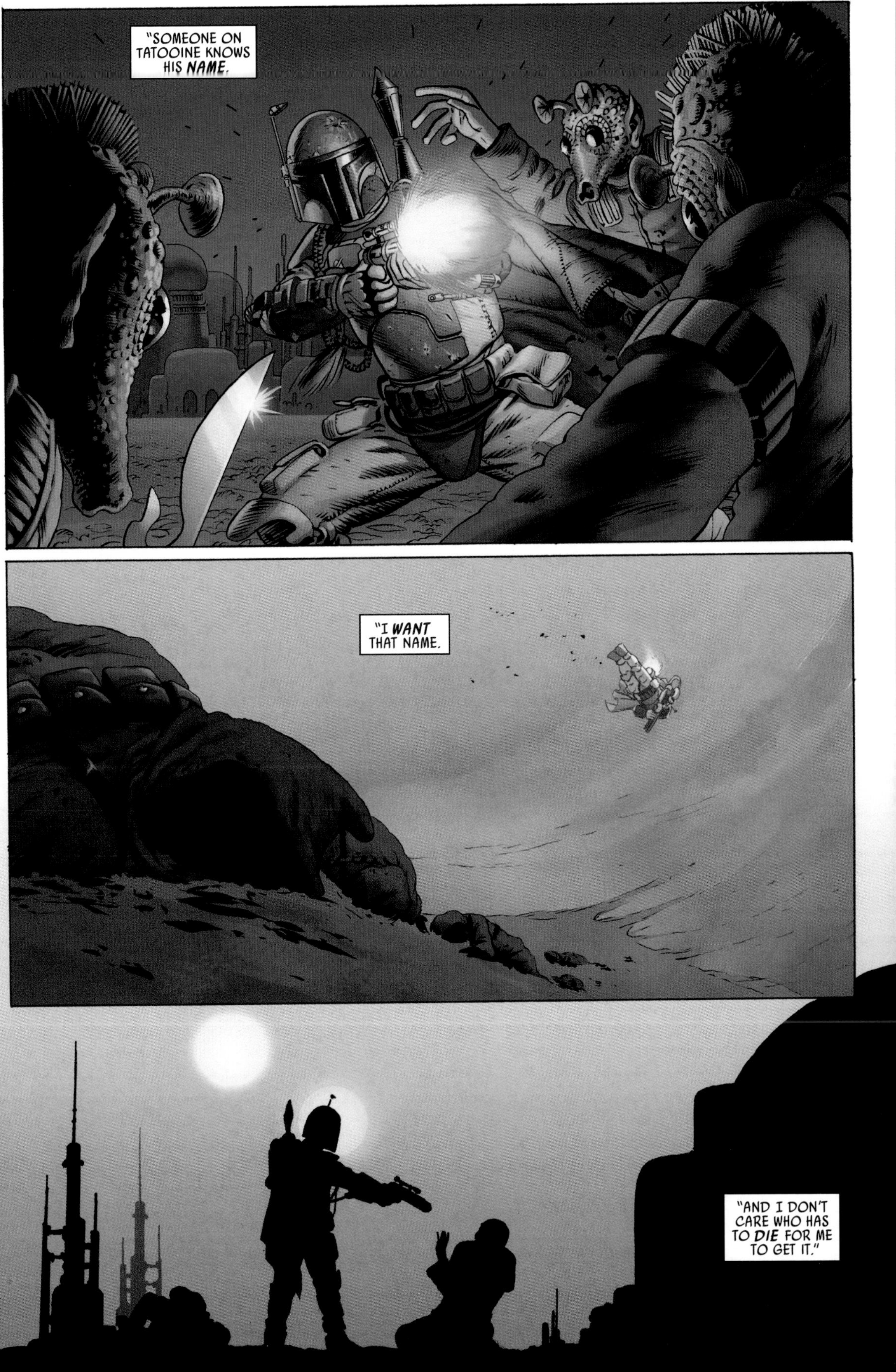
"SOMEONE ON TATOOINE KNOWS HIS NAME.
"I WANT THAT NAME.
"AND I DON'T CARE WHO HAS TO DIE FOR ME TO GET IT."

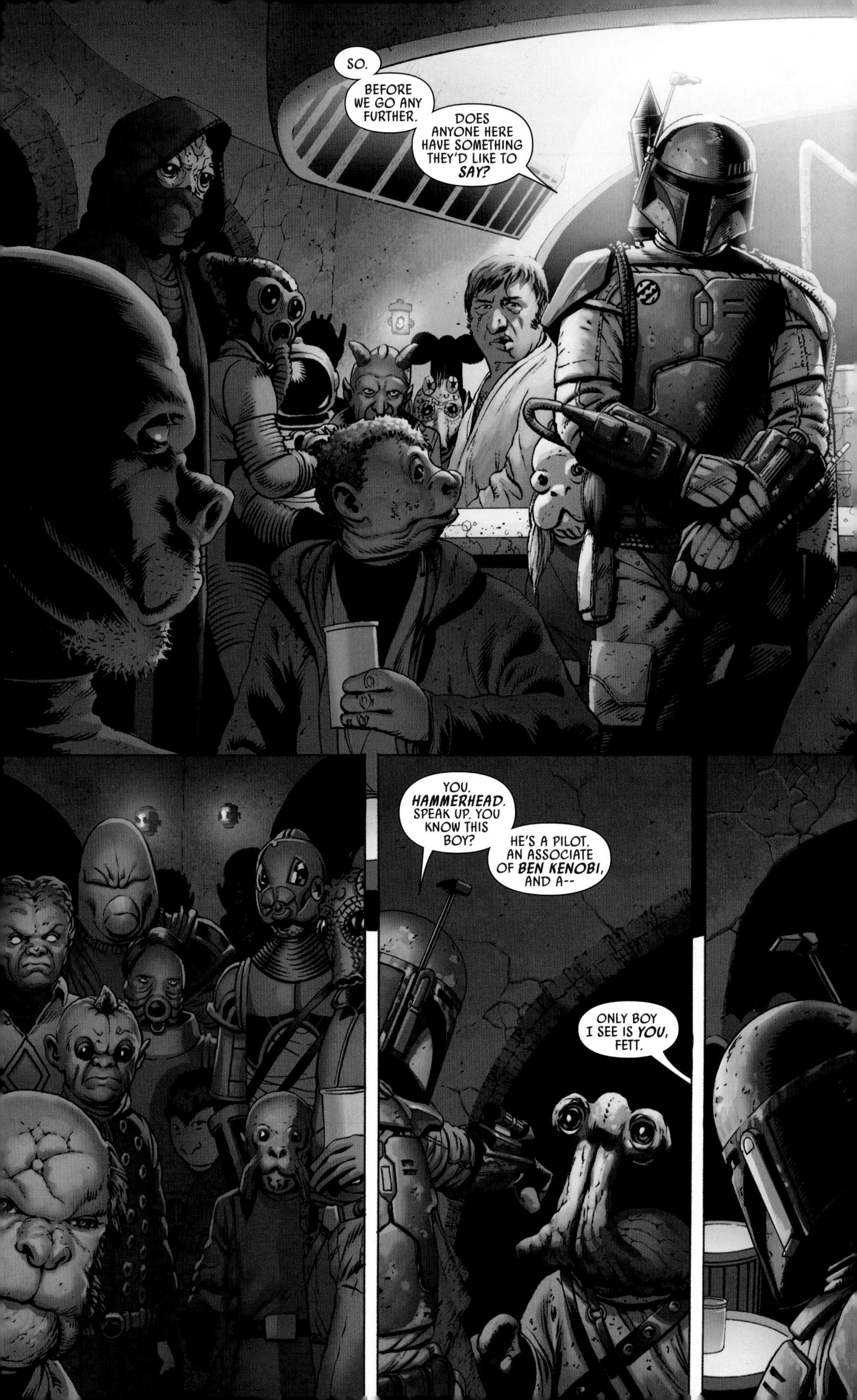
SO.
BEFORE WE GO ANY FURTHER.
DOES ANYONE HERE HAVE SOMETHING THEY'D LIKE TO SAY?
YOU. HAMMERHEAD. SPEAK UP. YOU KNOW THIS BOY?
HE'S A PILOT. AN ASSOCIATE OF BEN KENOBI, AND A--
ONLY BOY I SEE IS YOU, FETT.

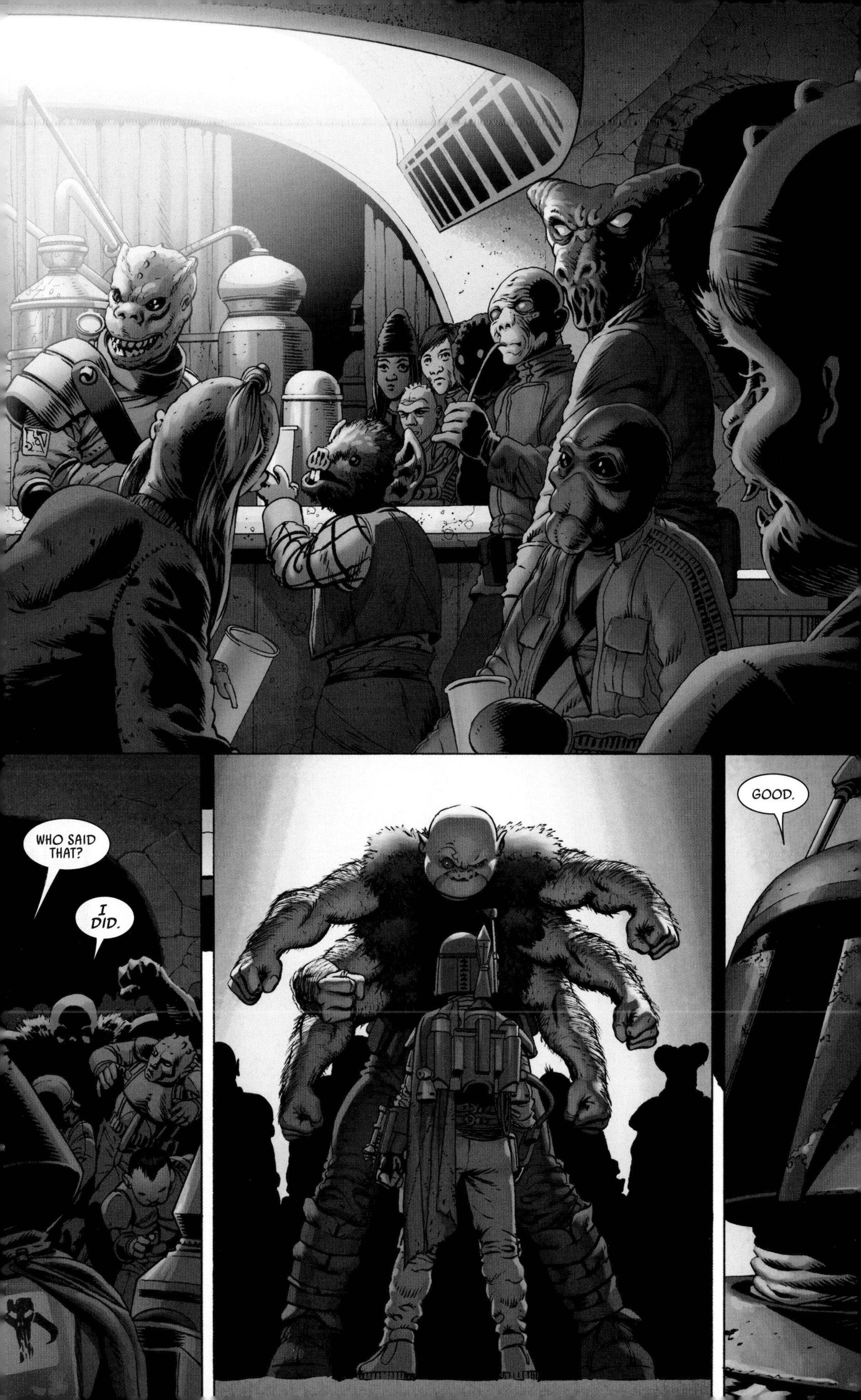
WHO SAID THAT?
I DID.
GOOD.

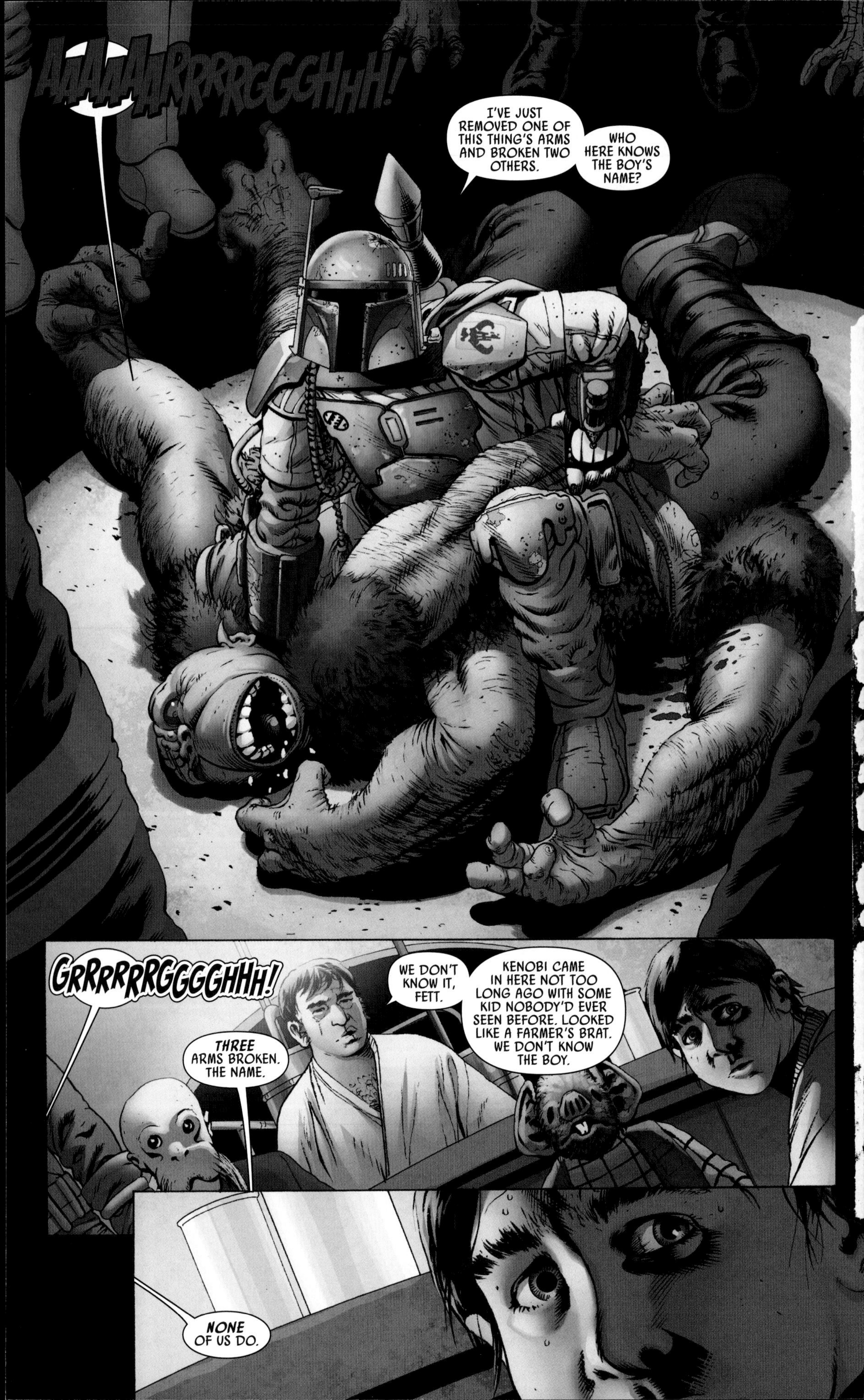
AAAAAARRRRGGGHHH!
I'VE JUST REMOVED ONE OF THIS THING'S ARMS AND BROKEN TWO OTHERS.
WHO HERE KNOWS THE BOY'S NAME?
GRRRRRRGGGGHHH!
THREE ARMS BROKEN. THE NAME.
WE DON'T KNOW IT, FETT.
KENOBI CAME IN HERE NOT TOO LONG AGO WITH SOME KID NOBODY'D EVER SEEN BEFORE. LOOKED LIKE A FARMER'S BRAT. WE DON'T KNOW THE BOY.
NONE OF US DO.

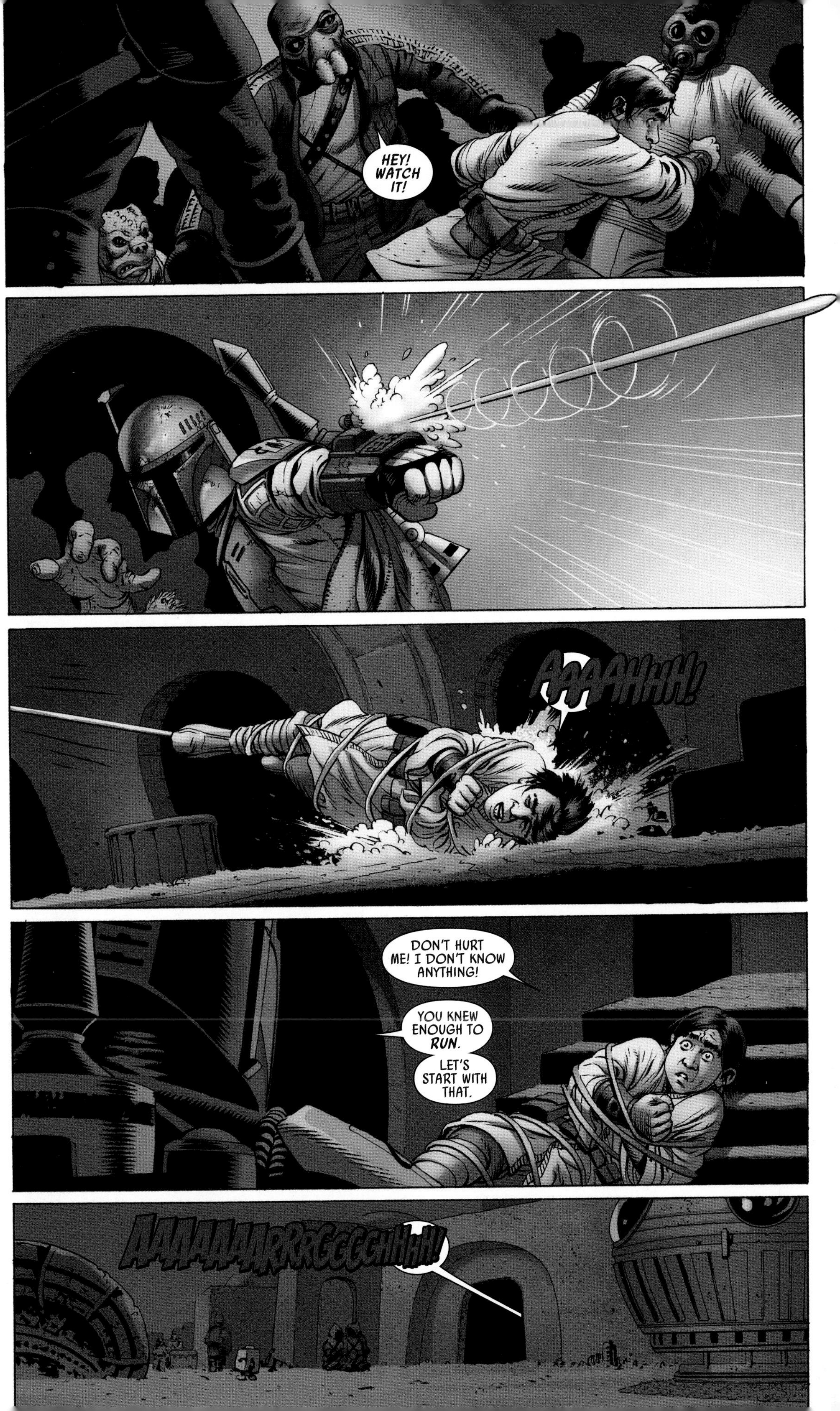
HEY! WATCH IT!
AAAAHHH!
DON'T HURT ME! I DON'T KNOW ANYTHING!
YOU KNEW ENOUGH TO RUN.
LET'S START WITH THAT.
AAAAAAARRRGGGGHHHH!

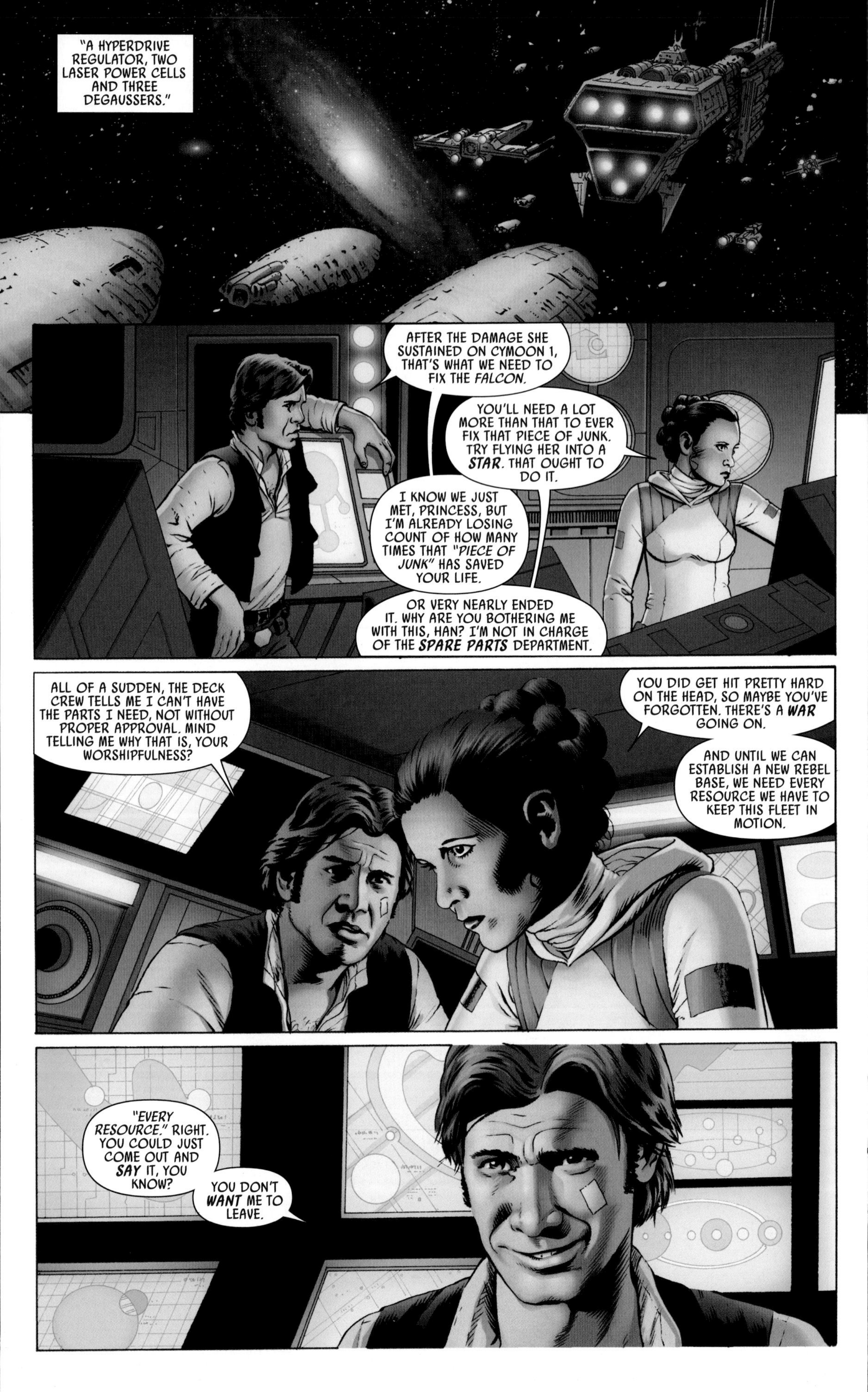
"A HYPERDRIVE REGULATOR, TWO LASER POWER CELLS AND THREE DEGAUSSERS."
AFTER THE DAMAGE SHE SUSTAINED ON CYMOON 1, THAT'S WHAT WE NEED TO FIX THE FALCON.
YOU'LL NEED A LOT MORE THAN THAT TO EVER FIX THAT PIECE OF JUNK. TRY FLYING HER INTO A STAR. THAT OUGHT TO DO IT.
I KNOW WE JUST MET, PRINCESS, BUT I'M ALREADY LOSING COUNT OF HOW MANY TIMES THAT "PIECE OF JUNK" HAS SAVED YOUR LIFE.
OR VERY NEARLY ENDED IT. WHY ARE YOU BOTHERING ME WITH THIS, HAN? I'M NOT IN CHARGE OF THE SPARE PARTS DEPARTMENT.
ALL OF A SUDDEN, THE DECK CREW TELLS ME I CAN'T HAVE THE PARTS I NEED, NOT WITHOUT PROPER APPROVAL. MIND TELLING ME WHY THAT IS, YOUR WORSHIPFULNESS?
YOU DID GET HIT PRETTY HARD ON THE HEAD, SO MAYBE YOU'VE FORGOTTEN. THERE'S A WAR GOING ON.
AND UNTIL WE CAN ESTABLISH A NEW REBEL BASE, WE NEED EVERY RESOURCE WE HAVE TO KEEP THIS FLEET IN MOTION.
"EVERY RESOURCE." RIGHT. YOU COULD JUST COME OUT AND SAY IT, YOU KNOW?
YOU DON'T WANT ME TO LEAVE.

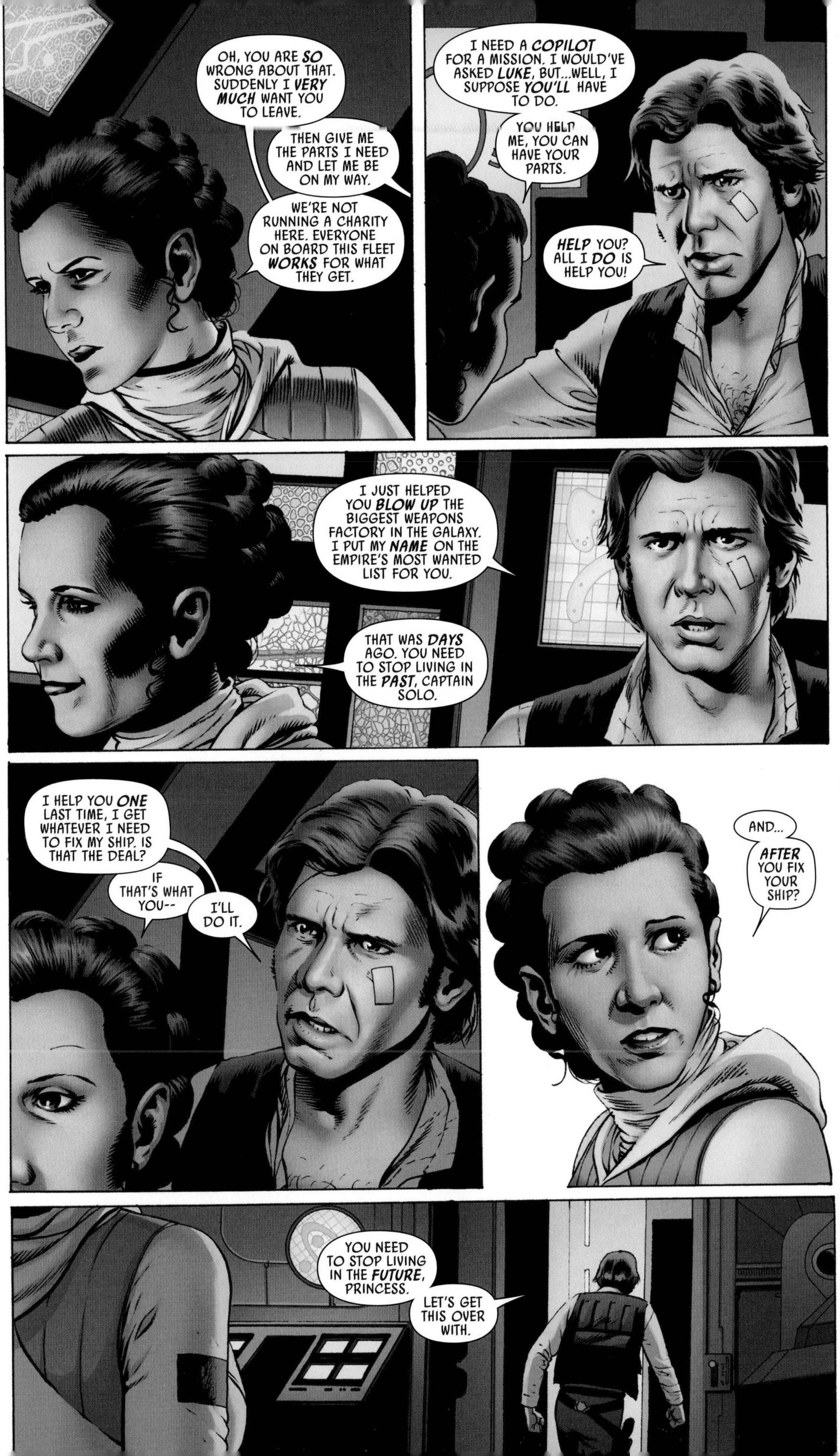
OH, YOU ARE SO WRONG ABOUT THAT. SUDDENLY I VERY MUCH WANT YOU TO LEAVE.
THEN GIVE ME THE PARTS I NEED AND LET ME BE ON MY WAY.
WE'RE NOT RUNNING A CHARITY HERE. EVERYONE ON BOARD THIS FLEET WORKS FOR WHAT THEY GET.
I NEED A COPILOT FOR A MISSION. I WOULD'VE ASKED LUKE, BUT...WELL, I SUPPOSE YOU'LL HAVE TO DO.
YOU HELP ME, YOU CAN HAVE YOUR PARTS.
HELP YOU? ALL I DO IS HELP YOU!
I JUST HELPED YOU BLOW UP THE BIGGEST WEAPONS FACTORY IN THE GALAXY. I PUT MY NAME ON THE EMPIRE'S MOST WANTED LIST FOR YOU.
THAT WAS DAYS AGO. YOU NEED TO STOP LIVING IN THE PAST, CAPTAIN SOLO.
I HELP YOU ONE LAST TIME, I GET WHATEVER I NEED TO FIX MY SHIP. IS THAT THE DEAL?
IF THAT'S WHAT YOU--
I'LL DO IT.
AND...
AFTER YOU FIX YOUR SHIP?
YOU NEED TO STOP LIVING IN THE FUTURE, PRINCESS.
LET'S GET THIS OVER WITH.

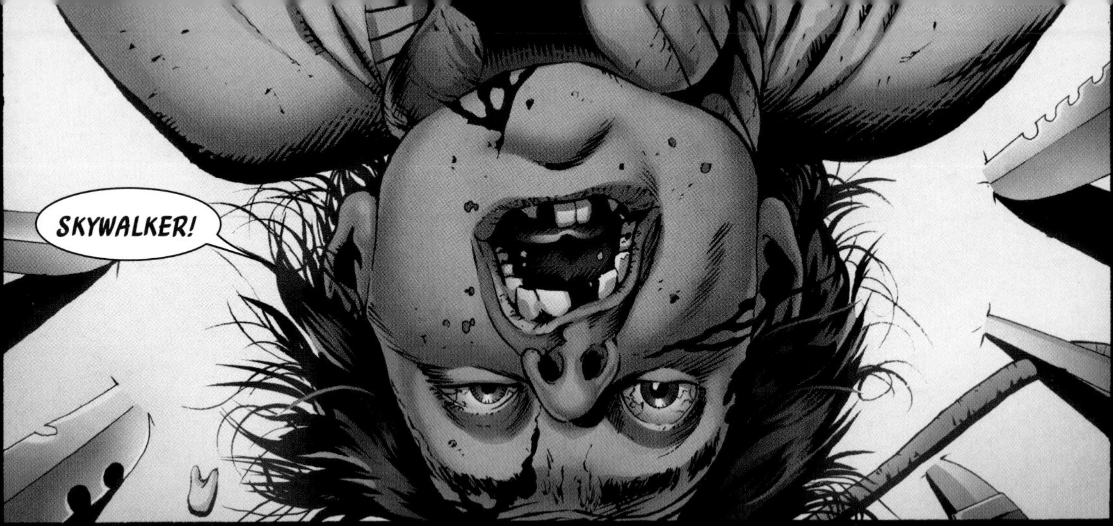
SKYWALKER!

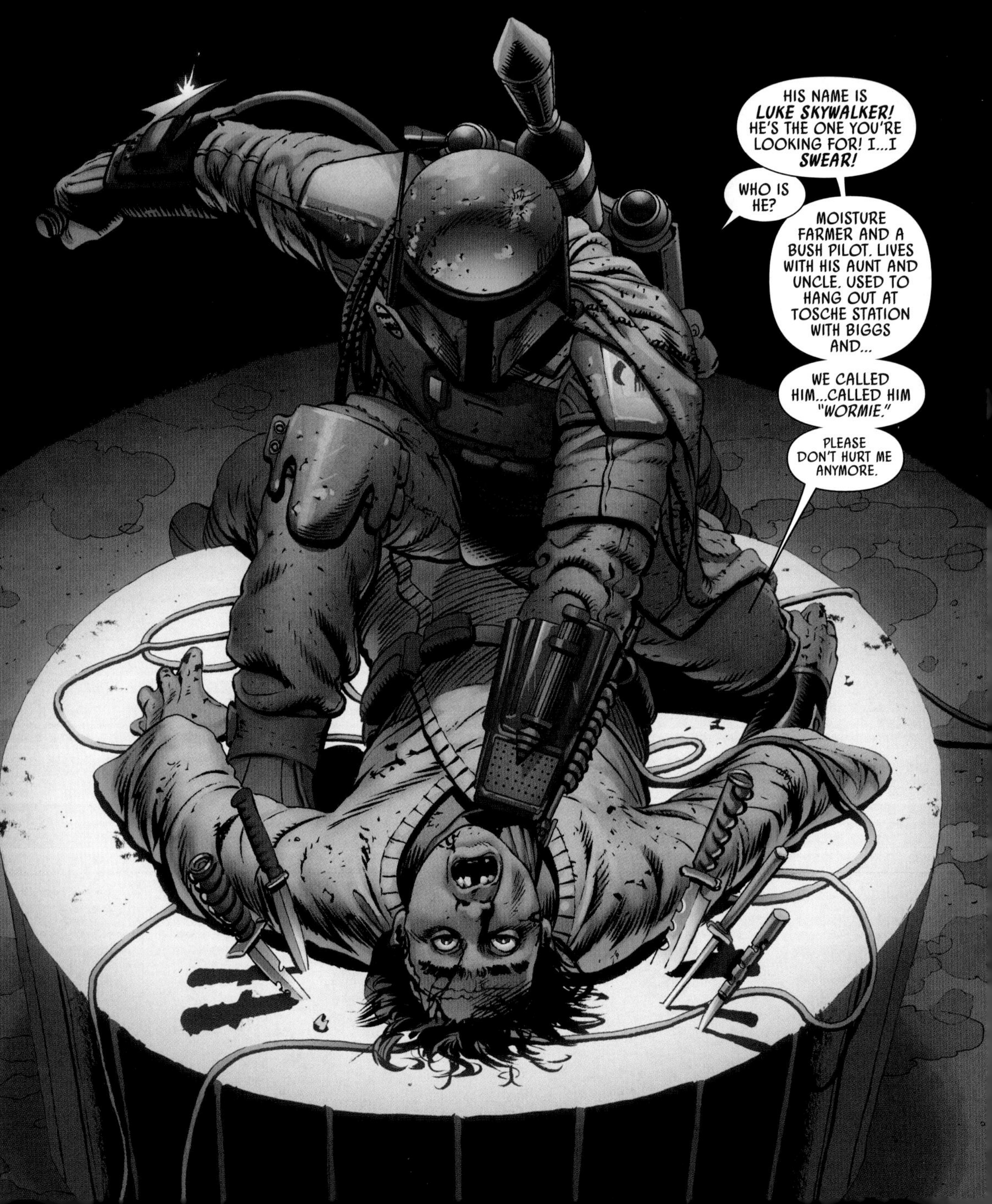
HIS NAME IS LUKE SKYWALKER! HE'S THE ONE YOU'RE LOOKING FOR! I...I SWEAR!
WHO IS HE?
MOISTURE FARMER AND A BUSH PILOT. LIVES WITH HIS AUNT AND UNCLE. USED TO HANG OUT AT TOSCHE STATION WITH BIGGS AND...
WE CALLED HIM...CALLED HIM "WORMIE."
PLEASE DON'T HURT ME ANYMORE.

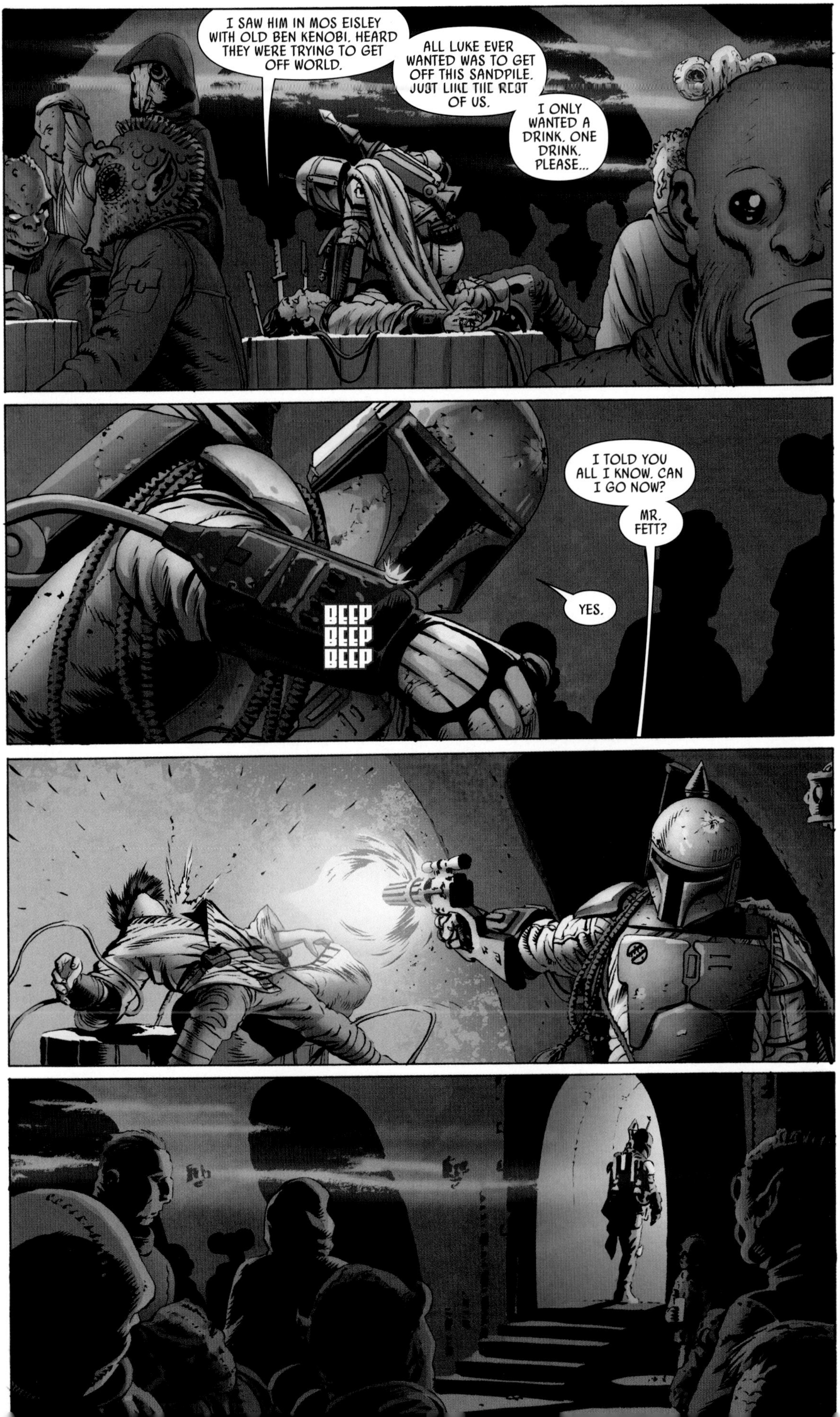
I SAW HIM IN MOS EISLEY WITH OLD BEN KENOBI. HEARD THEY WERE TRYING TO GET OFF WORLD.
ALL LUKE EVER WANTED WAS TO GET OFF THIS SANDPILE. JUST LIKE THE REST OF US.
I ONLY WANTED A DRINK. ONE DRINK. PLEASE...
I TOLD YOU ALL I KNOW. CAN I GO NOW?
MR. FETT?
BEEP BEEP BEEP
YES.

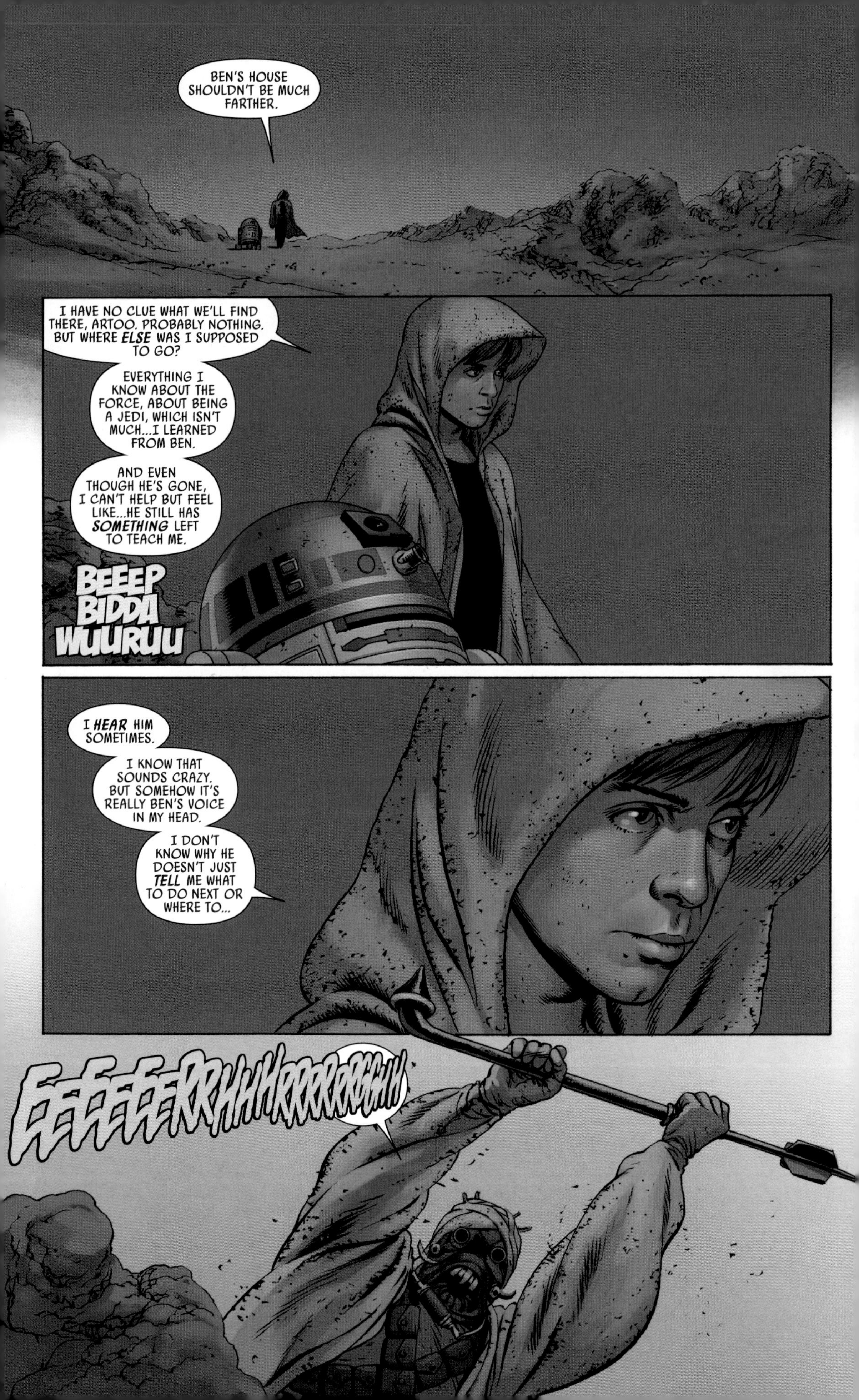
BEN'S HOUSE SHOULDN'T BE MUCH FARTHER.
I HAVE NO CLUE WHAT WE'LL FIND THERE, ARTOO. PROBABLY NOTHING. BUT WHERE ELSE WAS I SUPPOSED TO GO?
EVERYTHING I KNOW ABOUT THE FORCE, ABOUT BEING A JEDI, WHICH ISN'T MUCH...I LEARNED FROM BEN.
AND EVEN THOUGH HE'S GONE, I CAN'T HELP BUT FEEL LIKE...HE STILL HAS SOMETHING LEFT TO TEACH ME.
BEEEP BIDDA WUURUU
I HEAR HIM SOMETIMES.
I KNOW THAT SOUNDS CRAZY. BUT SOMEHOW IT'S REALLY BEN'S VOICE IN MY HEAD.
I DON'T KNOW WHY HE DOESN'T JUST TELL ME WHAT TO DO NEXT OR WHERE TO...
EEEEEERRHHHRRRRRRGHH

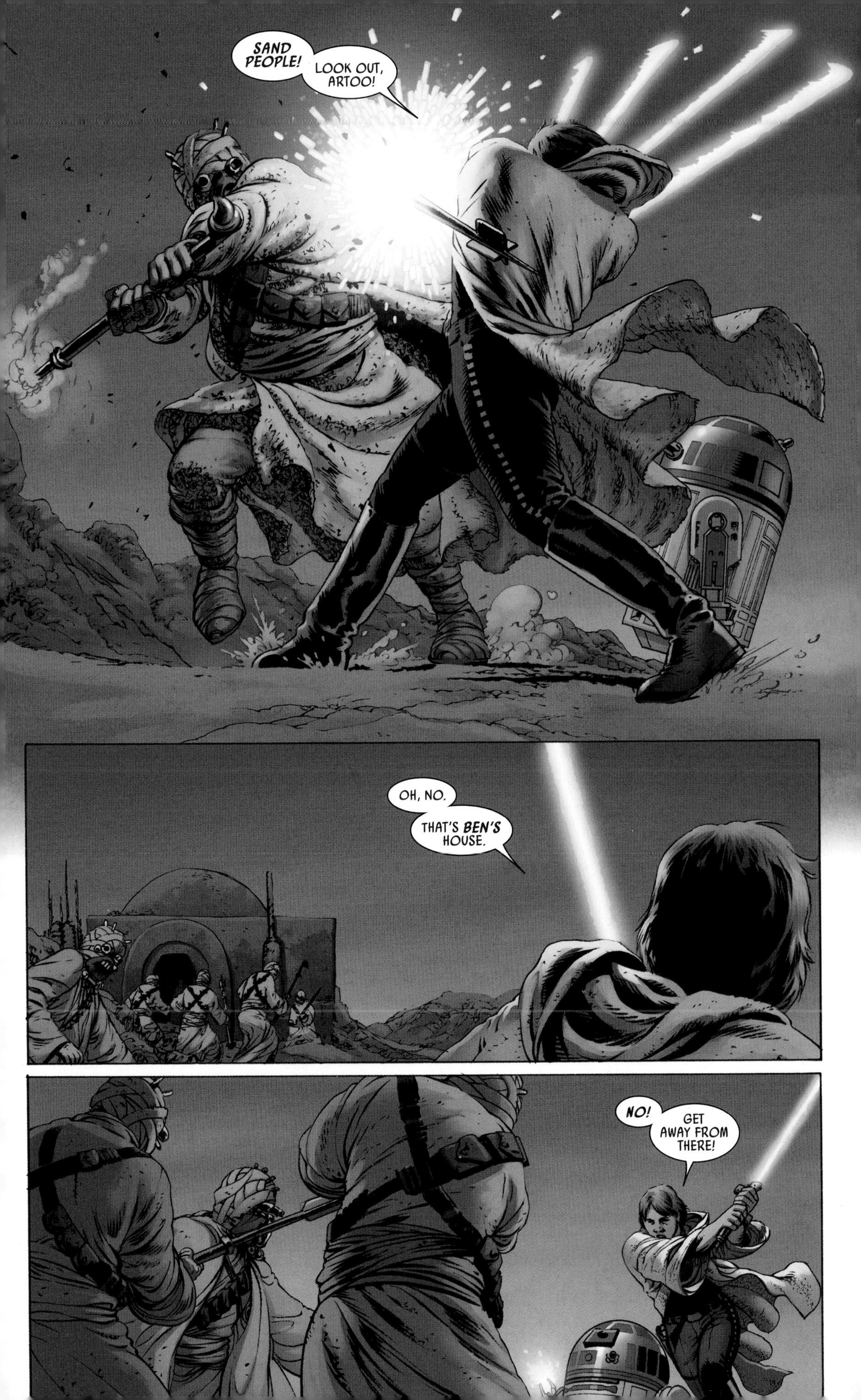
SAND PEOPLE!
LOOK OUT, ARTOO!
OH, NO.
THAT'S BEN'S HOUSE.
NO!
GET AWAY FROM THERE!

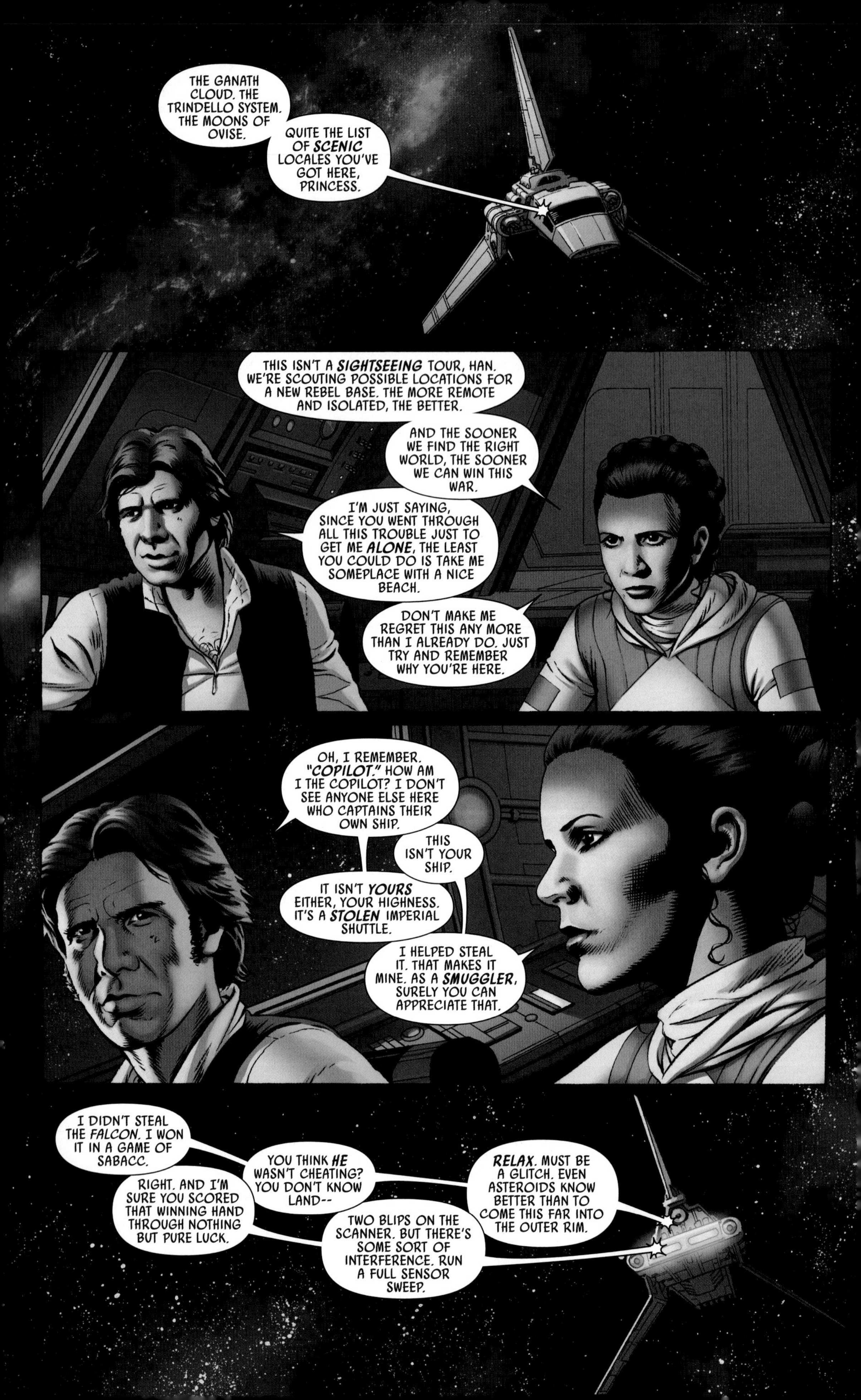

THE GANATH CLOUD. THE TRINDELLO SYSTEM. THE MOONS OF OVISE.
QUITE THE LIST OF *SCENIC* LOCALES YOU'VE GOT HERE, PRINCESS.
THIS ISN'T A *SIGHTSEEING* TOUR, HAN. WE'RE SCOUTING POSSIBLE LOCATIONS FOR A NEW REBEL BASE. THE MORE REMOTE AND ISOLATED, THE BETTER.
AND THE SOONER WE FIND THE RIGHT WORLD, THE SOONER WE CAN WIN THIS WAR.
I'M JUST SAYING, SINCE YOU WENT THROUGH ALL THIS TROUBLE JUST TO GET ME *ALONE*, THE LEAST YOU COULD DO IS TAKE ME SOMEPLACE WITH A NICE BEACH.
DON'T MAKE ME REGRET THIS ANY MORE THAN I ALREADY DO. JUST TRY AND REMEMBER WHY YOU'RE HERE.
OH, I REMEMBER. *"COPILOT."* HOW AM I THE COPILOT? I DON'T SEE ANYONE ELSE HERE WHO CAPTAINS THEIR OWN SHIP.
THIS ISN'T YOUR SHIP.
IT ISN'T *YOURS* EITHER, YOUR HIGHNESS. IT'S A *STOLEN* IMPERIAL SHUTTLE.
I HELPED STEAL IT. THAT MAKES IT MINE. AS A *SMUGGLER*, SURELY YOU CAN APPRECIATE THAT.
I DIDN'T STEAL THE *FALCON*. I WON IT IN A GAME OF SABACC.
RIGHT. AND I'M SURE YOU SCORED THAT WINNING HAND THROUGH NOTHING BUT PURE LUCK.
YOU THINK *HE* WASN'T CHEATING? YOU DON'T KNOW LAND--
TWO BLIPS ON THE SCANNER. BUT THERE'S SOME SORT OF INTERFERENCE. RUN A FULL SENSOR SWEEP.
RELAX. MUST BE A GLITCH. EVEN ASTEROIDS KNOW BETTER THAN TO COME THIS FAR INTO THE OUTER RIM.

ATTENTION, UNKNOWN SHUTTLE. YOU DO NOT HAVE CLEARANCE FOR THIS SECTOR.

IDENTIFY YOURSELF.

TIE FIGHTERS. YOU LET THEM STROLL RIGHT UP BEHIND US.

OKAY, I ADMIT IT, I'M A TERRIBLE COPILOT. NOW GIVE ME THE CONTROLS AND LET ME FLY US OUT OF THIS.

NO, RELAX. THIS IS WHY WE STOLE A SHUTTLE IN THE FIRST PLACE.

THIS IS SHUTTLE INVICTUS, OUT OF THE BLACKFEL SYSTEM, ON A CLASSIFIED SCOUTING MISSION.

TRANSMITTING CLEARANCE CODES NOW.

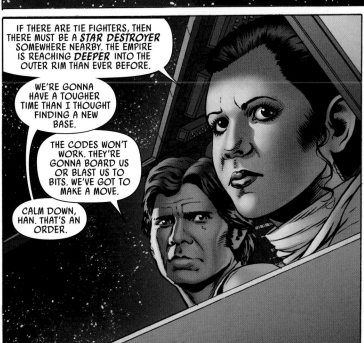

IF THERE ARE TIE FIGHTERS, THEN THERE MUST BE A STAR DESTROYER SOMEWHERE NEARBY. THE EMPIRE IS REACHING DEEPER INTO THE OUTER RIM THAN EVER BEFORE.

WE'RE GONNA HAVE A TOUGHER TIME THAN I THOUGHT FINDING A NEW BASE.

THE CODES WON'T WORK. THEY'RE GONNA BOARD US OR BLAST US TO BITS. WE'VE GOT TO MAKE A MOVE.

CALM DOWN, HAN. THAT'S AN ORDER.

SORRY, PRINCESS. YOU'LL THANK ME IN THE MORNING.

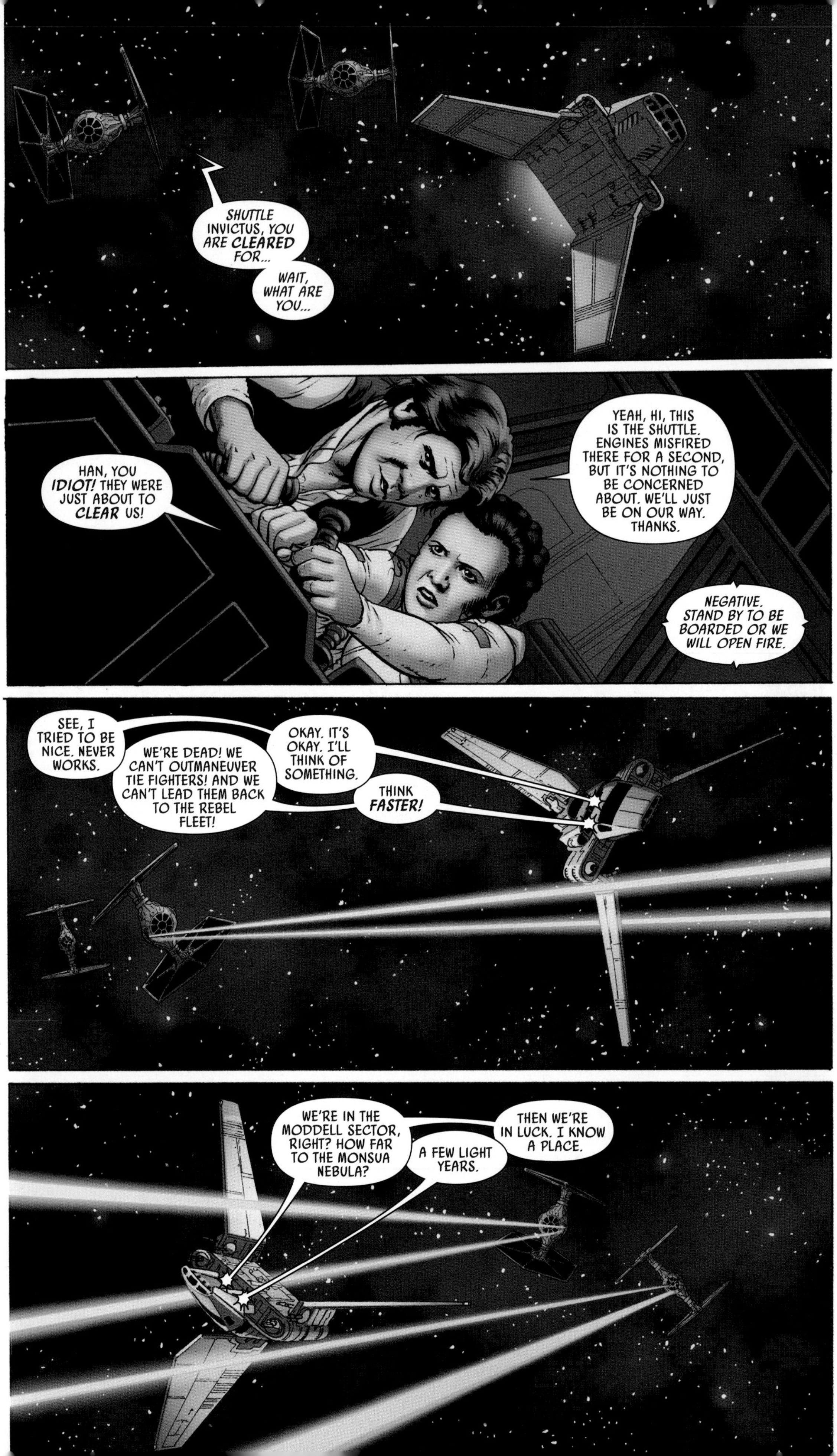

SHUTTLE INVICTUS, YOU ARE CLEARED FOR...
WAIT, WHAT ARE YOU...
HAN, YOU IDIOT! THEY WERE JUST ABOUT TO CLEAR US!
YEAH, HI, THIS IS THE SHUTTLE. ENGINES MISFIRED THERE FOR A SECOND, BUT IT'S NOTHING TO BE CONCERNED ABOUT. WE'LL JUST BE ON OUR WAY. THANKS.
NEGATIVE. STAND BY TO BE BOARDED OR WE WILL OPEN FIRE.
SEE, I TRIED TO BE NICE. NEVER WORKS.
WE'RE DEAD! WE CAN'T OUTMANEUVER TIE FIGHTERS! AND WE CAN'T LEAD THEM BACK TO THE REBEL FLEET!
OKAY. IT'S OKAY. I'LL THINK OF SOMETHING.
THINK FASTER!
WE'RE IN THE MODDELL SECTOR, RIGHT? HOW FAR TO THE MONSUA NEBULA?
A FEW LIGHT YEARS.
THEN WE'RE IN LUCK. I KNOW A PLACE.

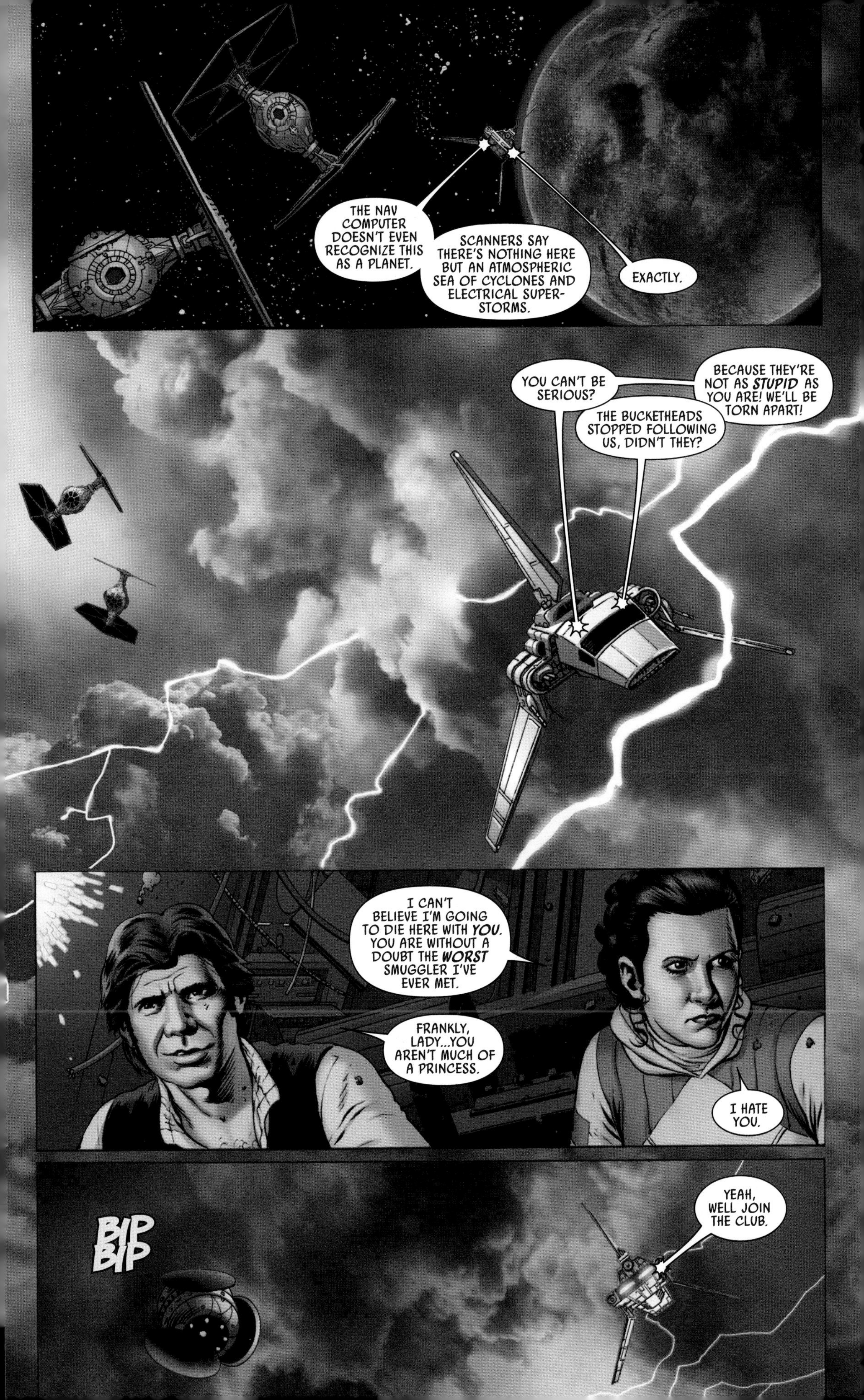
THE NAV COMPUTER DOESN'T EVEN RECOGNIZE THIS AS A PLANET.
SCANNERS SAY THERE'S NOTHING HERE BUT AN ATMOSPHERIC SEA OF CYCLONES AND ELECTRICAL SUPER-STORMS.
EXACTLY.
YOU CAN'T BE SERIOUS?
THE BUCKETHEADS STOPPED FOLLOWING US, DIDN'T THEY?
BECAUSE THEY'RE NOT AS STUPID AS YOU ARE! WE'LL BE TORN APART!
I CAN'T BELIEVE I'M GOING TO DIE HERE WITH YOU. YOU ARE WITHOUT A DOUBT THE WORST SMUGGLER I'VE EVER MET.
FRANKLY, LADY...YOU AREN'T MUCH OF A PRINCESS.
I HATE YOU.
YEAH, WELL JOIN THE CLUB.
BIP BIP

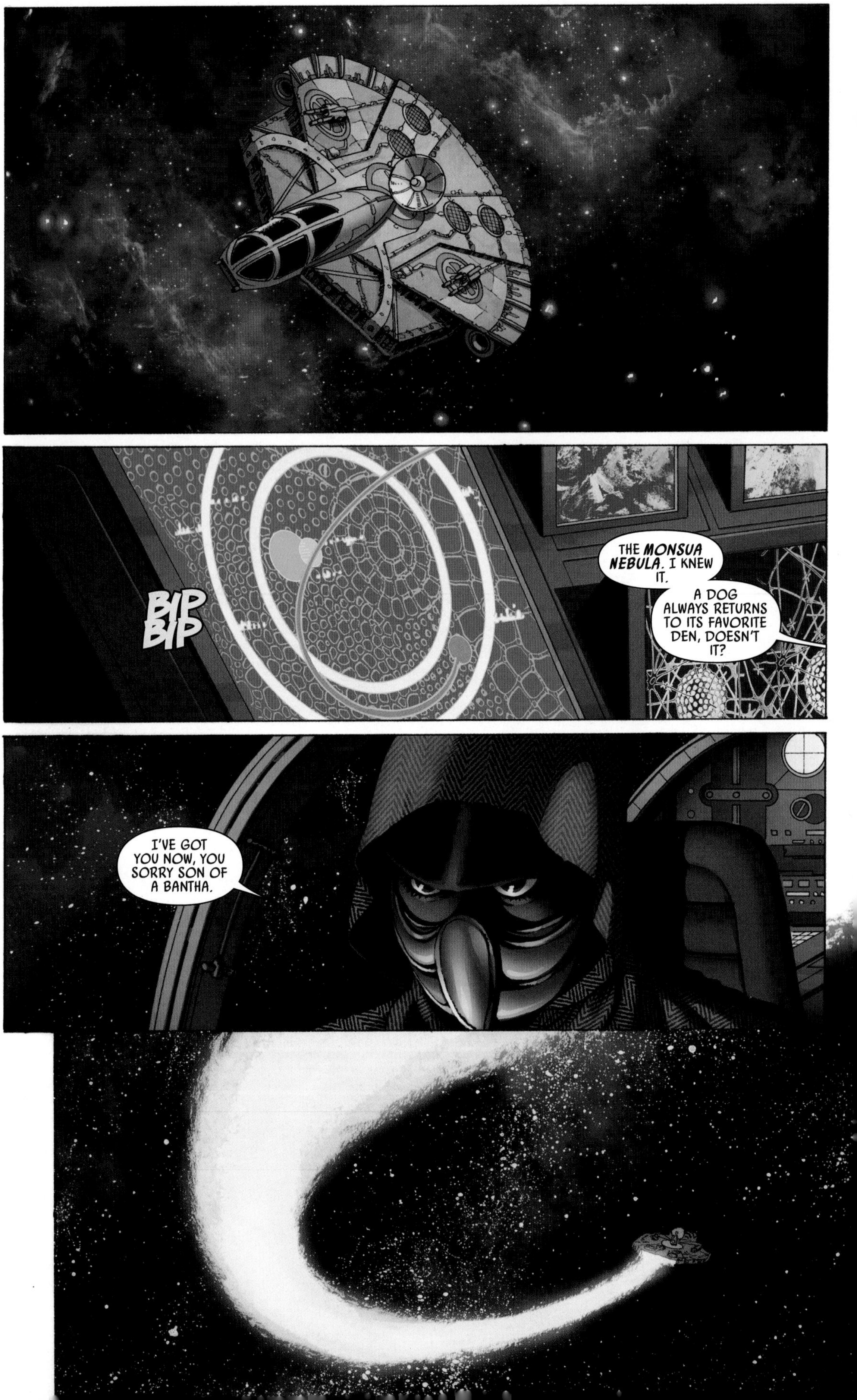
BIP BIP
THE MONSUA NEBULA. I KNEW IT.
A DOG ALWAYS RETURNS TO ITS FAVORITE DEN, DOESN'T IT?
I'VE GOT YOU NOW, YOU SORRY SON OF A BANTHA.

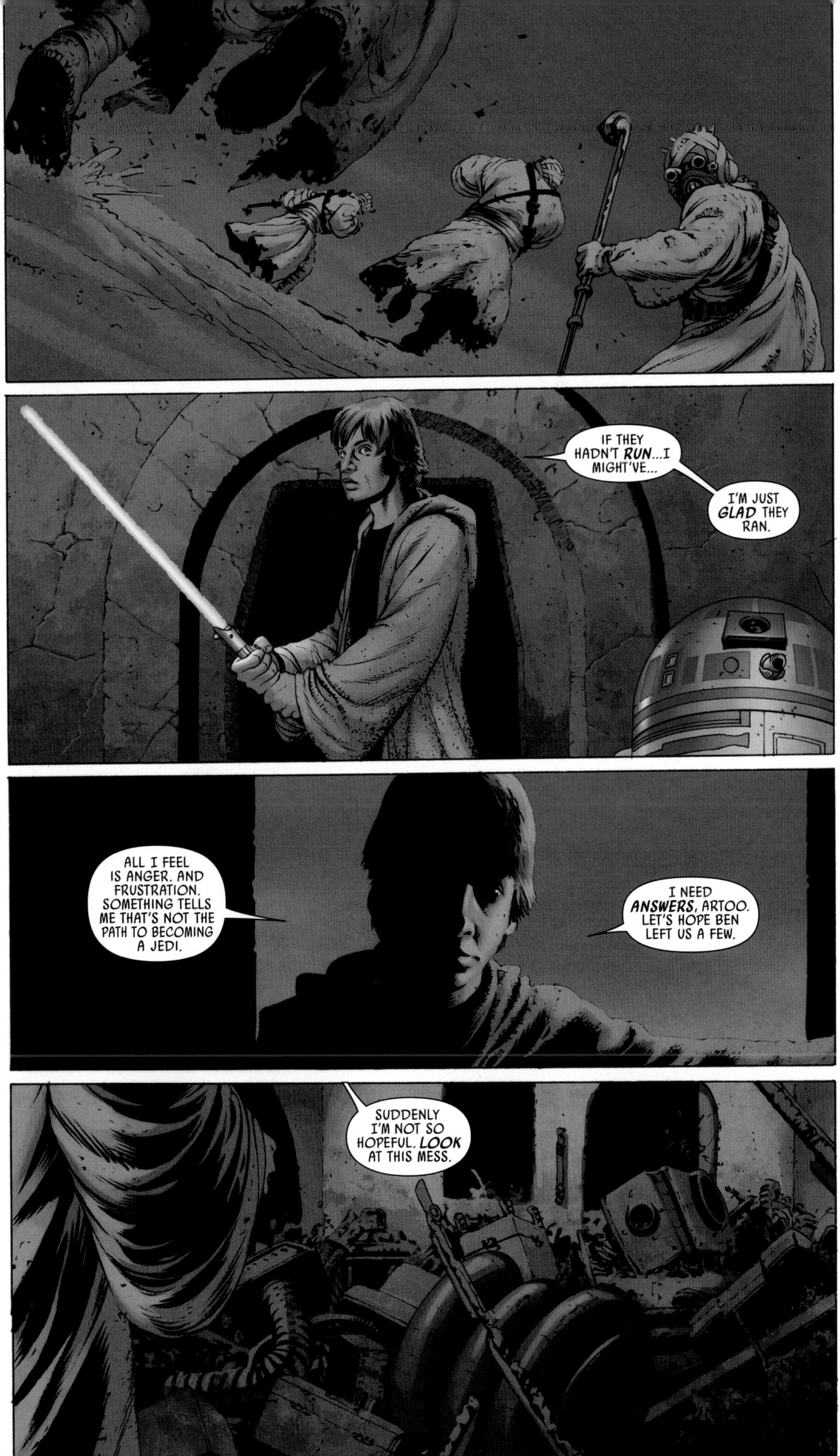
IF THEY HADN'T RUN...I MIGHT'VE...
I'M JUST GLAD THEY RAN.
ALL I FEEL IS ANGER. AND FRUSTRATION. SOMETHING TELLS ME THAT'S NOT THE PATH TO BECOMING A JEDI.
I NEED ANSWERS, ARTOO. LET'S HOPE BEN LEFT US A FEW.
SUDDENLY I'M NOT SO HOPEFUL. LOOK AT THIS MESS.

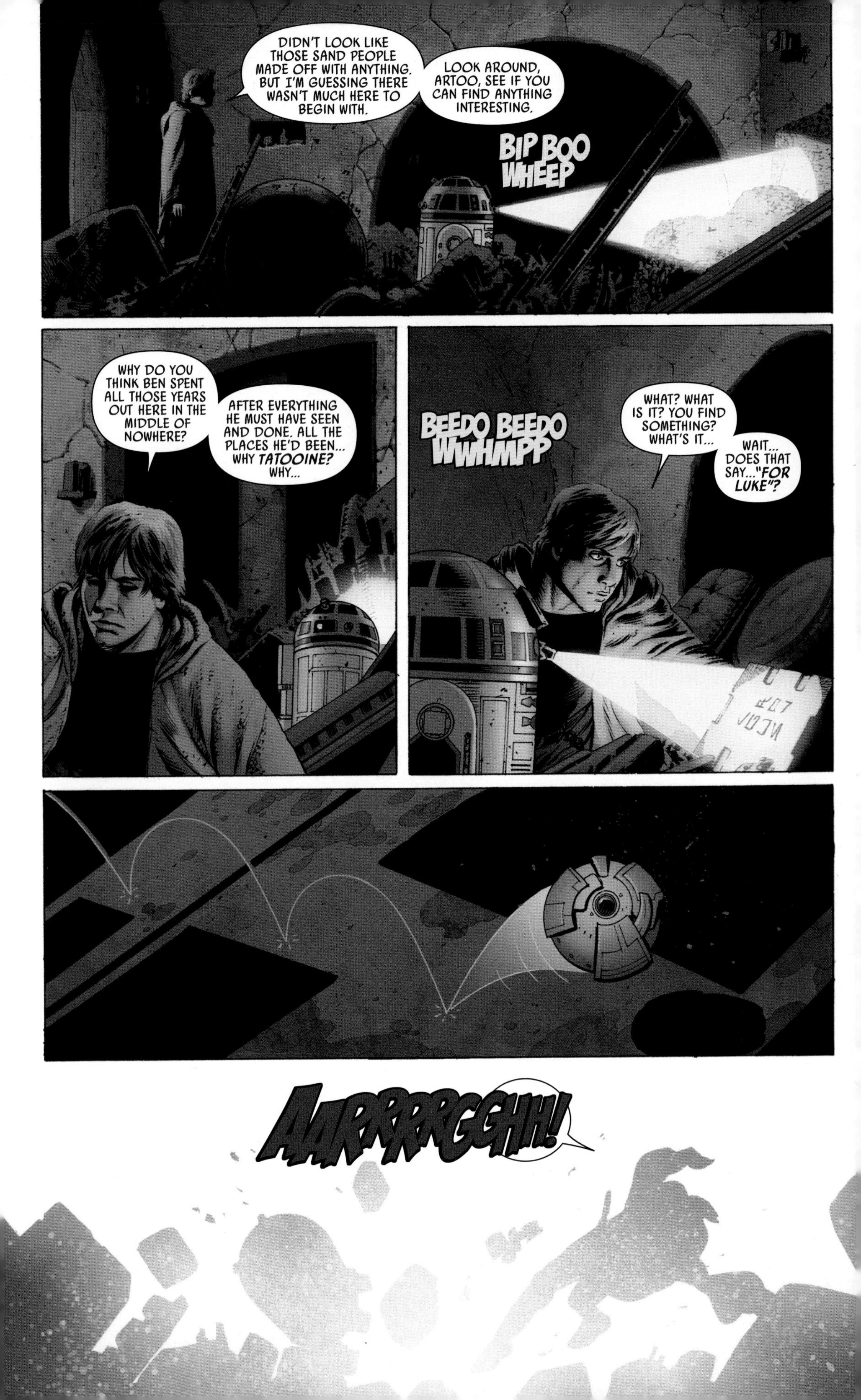
DIDN'T LOOK LIKE THOSE SAND PEOPLE MADE OFF WITH ANYTHING. BUT I'M GUESSING THERE WASN'T MUCH HERE TO BEGIN WITH.
LOOK AROUND, ARTOO, SEE IF YOU CAN FIND ANYTHING INTERESTING.
BIP BOO WHEEP
WHY DO YOU THINK BEN SPENT ALL THOSE YEARS OUT HERE IN THE MIDDLE OF NOWHERE?
AFTER EVERYTHING HE MUST HAVE SEEN AND DONE. ALL THE PLACES HE'D BEEN... WHY *TATOOINE?* WHY...
BEEDO BEEDO WWHMPP
WHAT? WHAT IS IT? YOU FIND SOMETHING? WHAT'S IT...
WAIT... DOES THAT SAY..."*FOR LUKE*"?
AARRRRRGGHH!

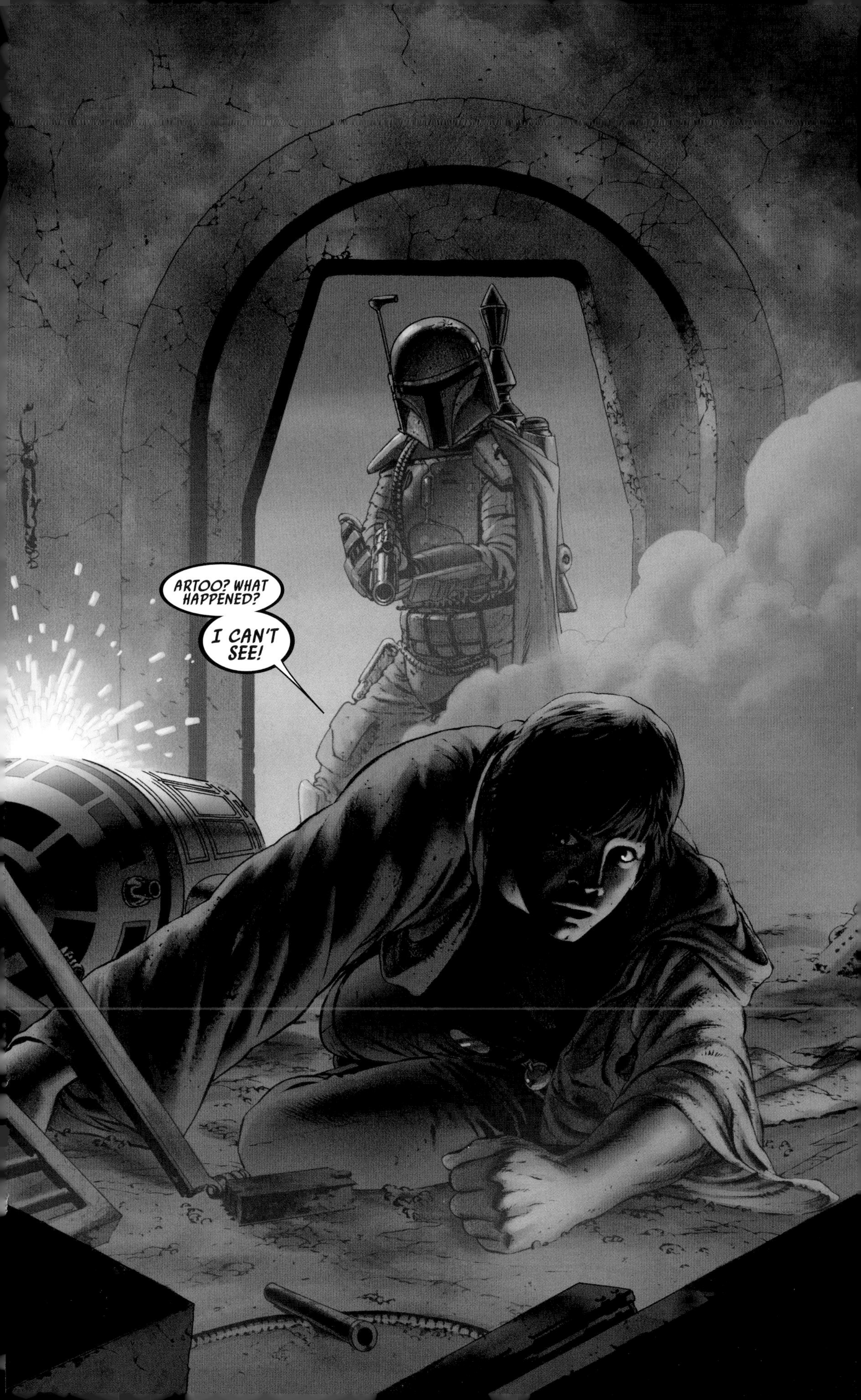
ARTOO? WHAT HAPPENED?
I CAN'T SEE!

SKYWALKER STRIKES

COLLECT THEM ALL!

Set of 6 Hardcover Books ISBN: 978-1-61479-526-1

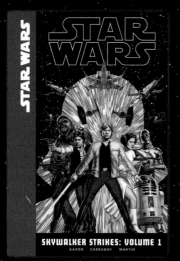

Hardcover Book ISBN
978-1-61479-527-8

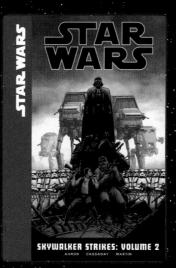

Hardcover Book ISBN
978-1-61479-528-5

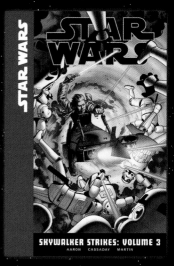

Hardcover Book ISBN
978-1-61479-529-2

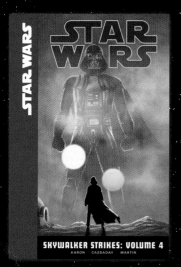

Hardcover Book ISBN
978-1-61479-530-8

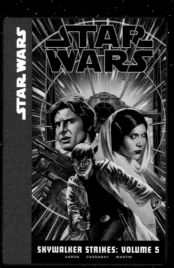

Hardcover Book ISBN
978-1-61479-531-5

Hardcover Book ISBN
978-1-61479-532-2